The
Roswell
Incident
1947

Dr Graham Clingbine

Disclaimer

This book is a review of the alleged crash-retrieval incident that occurred at Roswell (New Mexico) in 1947. It is based upon the author's interpretation and understanding of various sources of disclosed information. These sources may include books, articles, newspaper reports, documentaries and others such as Wikipedia. The degree of veracity of such sources of information is not prescribed or guaranteed nor the accuracy of quotations. For these reasons no references are given nor acknowledgements to any particular information source(s) in the body of this book. The content has been written in good faith and there is no intention to malign or misrepresent individuals, documentation or historical events.

However, the opinions, arguments, descriptions and ideas of the author may be reflected or referred to and are related to researched information. Information sources may have influenced the content presented in the script. Reference may be made in parts of the book to research studies and data collection. Where individual researchers are mentioned by name the information given is based on the opinion and reading done by the author. A great attempt has been made to report information accurately and the author apologises for any unintended misinformation or falsehood.

Any similarities in content to other published work is purely coincidental as there is no intent to plagiarise, misinform or undertake any form of malpractice.

The author is not legally liable for the ideas, opinions or factual veracity of information presented in the manuscript.

Published by:

Reed UK

ISBN: 978-1-8381919-0-0

Acknowledgement

Thank you to Lorraine Reed for designing the cover

ABOUT THE AUTHOR

Dr Graham Clingbine has BSc and MSc degrees from the University of London in the areas of Biological Science and Neurobiology. His award of PhD followed a research programme on the memory mechanisms of the brain. Dr Clingbine spent a long career in education at schools and colleges before retiring from City & Islington College in north London from his post as Senior Lecturer and Course Manager of the Medical Access course.

Dr Clingbine has co-authored a number of paperback books related to model answers to biology examination questions prior to writing his more recent book publications. He has a keen interest and extensive research knowledge in the subject area of unidentified flying objects (UFOs) and related phenomena including alien abductions and alleged secret governmental conspiracy theories which may cover-up cases of alien contact.

Dr Clingbine has a number of interests and hobbies but uppermost among these is fishing. He not only enjoys fishing the rivers, lakes and seas of his home country (the UK) but has ventured further afield to countries across Europe and the USA.

Contents

Chapter 1
Foreward

The truth is out there – hiding in plain sight

Strange aerial sightings, anomalous entities and inexplicable discoveries have been observed since antiquity, perhaps from before recorded history. If it is not all mass hysteria, illusion or hallucination, where should we start looking to explain such phenomena? Here are just a **FEW** places and subjects readers can research.

Folklore, myths and legends – examples are: the green children of Woolpit, out of place time-travel photos such as those known as Charlie Chaplin's time traveller (1928), the modern day hipster (1941) and the mobile phone user (1943)

Ancient rock paintings and art

Ancient cave paintings

Sumeria and cuneiform clay writing

Ancient Egyptian pyramids (such as The Great Pyramid of Giza, aka The Pyramid of Khufu and The Pyramid of Cheops) – **hieroglyphs**

The ancient Mayan civilisation, temples, pyramids

The lost continent of **Atlantis**

The Bible, Quran and other Holy Scriptures: Biblical examples include the Ark of the Covenant - the Book of Genesis, the Book of Ezekiel, the Book of Enoch, Ascension into Heaven

Noah and the Great Flood

Jinns

Vimanas

Elohim

Nephilim (Watchers)

Annunaki

Angels

The Mahabharata

Observations and records made by soldiers and scholars of the **Roman Empire**

Medieval paintings showing ''UFOs''

Inexplicable or strange ancient and more recent **artefacts and sites** – the Piri Reis Map (compiled 1513), the Voynich Manuscript (compiled 15th century), the Baghdad Battery (dates back about 1,800 years, discovered 1936), Dropa stones (date back 12,000 years, discovered 1938), crystal skulls (estimates range from 5,000 to 36,000 years old), Stonehenge (3,000 BC to 2,000 BC), Easter Island Moai (1,250 to 1,500 years old)

The Nuremberg Aerial UFO Battle (1561)

Cryptid creatures – mothman (1966), chupacabra (1995)

Crop circles

Cattle and other mutilations

Nazca lines, glyphs and representations visible from space

Dogon tribal mythology and the *Sirius* binary star system (1930)

The Black Knight satellite (1954)

The Baltic Sea Anomaly (2011)

Angel hair

The Arecibo Message (1974)

The WOW signal (1977)

Mystery Airships (1896/1897)

Ghost and rocket ships (1946)

UAPs – unexplained aerial phenomena: the Norway Spiral (2009)

Some Fairly Recent Historical events – a **FEW** examples are the Battle of Los Angeles (1942), the Kenneth Arnold sighting of 'flying saucers' (1947), the Lubbock lights (1951), the Washington flap (1952), the Lonnie Zamora sighting (1964), the Colares flap (1977), the Rendlesham Forest incident (RAF Woodbridge and Bentwaters 1980), the Gulf Breeze incident (1987), the Voronezh UFO landing incident (1989), the Belgian Wave (1989/1990), the Mexican Waves (1991 to 1994), the Cosford incident (1993), the Zimbabwe UFO landing at the Ariel Elementary School (1994), the Phoenix lights (1997)

UFO sightings (unidentified flying objects/flying saucers) evidence from: witness accounts and drawings - sworn testimonies and deathbed confessions - pilot and ship captains accounts, logs and video recordings - military reports - radar contacts - police reports - governmental reports and investigations (like Project Blue Book, the Condon Report) - foo fighters - possible Nazi UFOs such as *Die Glocke/The Bell* - alleged UFO crashes - cases of suspected UFO retrievals and back-engineering - governmental secrecy, cover-ups and misinformation - military programmes and top secret bases - recordings on videos, camcorders and photos of anomalous entity and UFO sightings - experiences of Presidents of the USA made public - mysterious governmental committees (such as the Majestic 12/MJ12) and agents (like the 'Men in Black') - anomalous recordings of objects observed in space from space stations, on the moon, on Mars - space signals - newly discovered Earth-like planets and other interstellar unexplained phenomena - the rapid advance of advanced technology (such as with silicon chips, artificial intelligence, robotics and nanotechnology)

USO sightings (unidentified submerged objects) evidence: as above for UFOs but including the Christopher Columbus Submerged Object Observation (1492) - the Shag Harbour incident (1967)

Alleged UFO crashes – the Aurora crash (1897), the crash at Cape Girardeau (1941), the Roswell crash (1947), the Kingman crash (1953), the Kecksburg crash (1965)

Controversial military bases associated with conspiracy theories related to extraterrestrial contact, reverse-engineering projects and UFO sightings - Wright Field/ Wright Patterson Air Base, Fort Hood, Kasputin Yar, Area 51 (Groom Lake or Dreamland), Papoose Lake (Area S4), Dulce Base, Dugway Proving Ground, Pine Gap

Secretive research carried out with possible governmental support or funding – Skunk Works (Lockheed Martin)

Modern scientific knowledge of fundamental sub-atomic particles, string theory, black and white holes, dark matter and dark energy, the likelihood of multi-dimensions and multi-universes, the Einsteinian interpretation of relativity and the slowing of time as the speed of light is approached

Body implants of unknown origin and function

Accounts of **contactees** and **close encounters** – the Hopkinsville Goblins case (1955), George Adamski (born 1891- died 1965), Billy Meier (1970s), Betty Andreasson Luca (1967), Whitley Strieber (1990s)

Accounts of **abductees** – Antonio Vilas-Boas (born 1934 – died 1991), Betty and Barney Hill (1961), Travis Walton (1975), the Allagash abduction (1976)

Retrieved abduction memories under hypnosis

Whistleblowers – Phil Schneider (1954 and 1979), Charles Hall (1967), Donna Hare (1970s), Bob Lazar (1980s), Gary McKinnon (2002), Paul Hellyer (2005)

Missing aircraft and pilot fatalities - Thomas Mantell's death (1948), Frederick Valentich's disappearance (1978)

UFO sightings by astronauts and cosmonauts

So… what kind of theories might account for UFOs and EBEs (Extraterrestrial Biological Entities)?

Let's put to one side religious beliefs, paranormal encounters, myths, delusions and paranoia etc. Some other possible explanations include…

Extraterresrial visitation

Interdimensional jumps

Time travel

So… what kinds of technological propulsion systems might be relevant to exotic travel and sightings? A few examples are…

Solar sails

Alcubiere Drives

Warping spacetime

Teleportation

Matter-antimatter engines

Nuclear fusion engines

Stargates

Portals

Traversable wormholes

Readers are invited to research the above-quoted examples for themselves or read further details in my book **UFO Sightings And Alien Abductions And Other Strange Related Events.**

Chapter 2
1947

A Landmark Year in Modern Ufology

1947 may not spring to mind as a year of particular importance. Yet it would turn out to be a historical landmark in the enigmatic subject area that is now known widely as Ufology. Various events occurred which resulted in this fateful year now being hailed as the beginning of the modern era of the study of unidentified flying objects.

Let's briefly step back in time. There had been numerous historical accounts of strange objects being observed in the skies and also landings of anomalous craft dating back to antiquity. In addition, numerous inexplicable artefacts had been discovered and there was evidence of strange lost civilisations such as those in Sumeria, ancient Egypt and on the South American mainland where Mayan remains were discovered.

Some of these ancient cultures possessed surprisingly high levels of scientific knowledge. This knowledge included astronomical alignments of complex buildings like pyramids and temples with star systems and the production of accurate calendars.

Ancient civilisations commonly produced hieroglyphs and writings which have been translated and interpreted. One common thread linking these societies relates to Gods descending from the stars or heavens in various types of craft. It is possible that these so-called Gods were extraterrestrials.

There are also ancient visual representations which nowadays would be described as resembling modern day aircraft, helicopters and rockets. Strange-looking beings are also drawn and these have produced a field of contemporary discussion which is referred to these days as studies of *ancient astronauts*.

Numerous accounts in religious texts describe what might be thought of as supernatural events. These may be mythological but there is a possibility that the scribes and authors of the time recorded what they actually saw. In those days it would have been impossible to grasp the concept of aerial craft and exotic beings and such observations would have been described in the terminology of the day. Descriptions of Gods and chariots and so on were recorded in an attempt to understand what had been observed.

Prior to 1947, a Mexican astronomer named Jose Bonilla took probably what was the earliest photo of UFOs. This was recorded on the 12th August 1883. He was studying sunspot activity at the *Zacatecas Observatory* when he observed 300 unknown objects pass across the field of view. These objects were captured on photographs after he exposed the wet plates. Various explanations were suggested for the pictures such as overflying geese and parts of a comet passing by the Earth.

An alleged UFO crash had already been documented before 1947. This occurred at Aurora in Texas in 1897. A strange airship apparently crashed into a windmill and the pilot was killed and buried by the local townspeople. The deceased occupant of the craft was described as being *not of this world* and *a Martian*.

Waves of phantom airship sightings were reported across the USA during 1896 and 1897. Crews were often human-looking. They waved and shouted down to onlookers saying that they were from Mars.

1946 was a year during which numerous strange reports emanated from Scandinavia. Objects resembling missiles were observed flying over the skies of countries such as Sweden. These objects showed some variation to each other. For example, some appeared to have wings while others did not. Over 2,000 sightings were reported. Some of these sightings gave radar returns but not all of them. These strange UFOs came to be known as *Ghost Rockets*.

Attempts were made to explain these sightings away as meteor trails. Other explanations related them to the recent ending of World War 2 in 1945. It was proposed that the objects were wartime VI or V2 rockets being tested by the Russian military. However, these Ghost Rockets often travelled in formations or groups and moved relatively slowly. No exhaust trails were observed and even more strangely they emitted no noise. Oddly, these objects were frequently observed to crash down into lakes in what appeared to be a controlled manner and disappear below the surface. Debris would never be found nor any objects retrieved.

1947 finally arrived. It was not a relaxed period as this year heralded the beginning of the *Cold War*. The political tensions that this created continued all the way through to 1991 at which point the Soviet Union dissolved into its component parts.

The Cold War produced rivalries between the USA and its allies and the Soviet Union and their allies. Many countries became part of western and eastern blocs with the so-called *iron curtain* separating them. Sir Winston Churchill used this term in September of 1947 during a meeting attended by communist leaders in Szklarska Poreba in Poland. The wartime leader Joseph Stalin did not attend the meeting in person but sent a representative. During this period, Harry S. Truman served as the 33rd President of the United States having succeeded Franklin D. Roosevelt in 1945.

The two bloc rivals mistrusted each other and there was resultant secrecy and spying which continued for many years after 1947. The two superpowers supported proxy wars in regional conflicts in an effort to achieve global influence. The ideological concept of *mutually assured destruction* ensured that both sides did not deploy their nuclear arsenals against each other. The rivalry extended to the *Space Race* in order to beat the opposing side to venture into and make use of outer space.

It is interesting to note that President Truman was not only involved with establishing NATO as a military defensive alliance but he was in office during governmental UFO investigations such as Projects Sign, Grudge and Blue Book. The latter was set up in March 1952 to determine if UFOs were a threat to national security.

However during 1947, Truman was also allegedly involved with forming a top secret committee referred to as the Majestic12 or Magic 12/MJ12 to covertly facilitate the recovery, investigation and studies of alien spacecraft. The group is said to have consisted of scientists, military personnel and government officials.

The general events of 1947 followed the common patterns of daily life. There were heavy falls of snow in the UK and Canada in January and various disastrous accidents occurred such as an awful train crash in Japan which killed 184 people in February. In the same month a notable launch into space took place with a V2 rocket known as *Blossom 1*. This was part of a US Army Ordnance Corps programme referred to as *Hermes*. The first animals were sent up into space. The cargo included fruit flies and various plants.

In March a German rocket scientist who was to become an important part of the NASA organisation married Maria von Quirstorp. The scientist was Wernher von Braun.

During this period President Truman in the USA pledged to prevent the spread of communism. The progression of March into April saw the announcement that Bedouin shepherds had discovered ancient religious texts in the Qumran Caves that later became known as the *Dead Sea Scrolls*.

During May some airline crashes occurred but the arrival of June brought some interesting events into the public domain. One of these events was a report by a seaman named Harold Dahl. He claimed to have observed six unusual unidentified flying objects (UFOs) over Puget Sound (Washington) in the vicinity of Maury Island. This occurred on or about June 21st. Dahl also reported an encounter the next day with persons unknown that today would be called *Men in Black*.

Just three days after the Dahl incident came a milestone event in UFO history. On June 24th pilot Kenneth Arnold described observations of unknown exotic craft flying over the Cascade mountains near Mount Rainier in Washington State. His description of the encounter led to the term *flying saucers* entering the vocabulary of popular culture. These observations are discussed more fully later.

The main subject matter of this book came into being on July 8th. A crashed (and recovered) *flying disc* was reported by the press at a ranch in Roswell (New Mexico). Alien bodies were said to have been retrieved and at least one was purportedly still alive after the crash. The story was later changed and the crashed craft was said to have actually been a weather balloon.

Political events continued through August following the partition of parts of the Indian sub-continent with India achieving independence from the British Empire.

In September typhoons and hurricanes hit Japan and the USA with many deaths. In October the word *computer* was used to describe electronic digital machinery and Captain Chuck Yeager piloted a Bell X-1 aircraft faster than the speed of sound.

November is notable for a number of events. On November 20th in the UK, Princess Elizabeth (Queen Elizabeth 2nd) married Prince Philip (the Duke of Edinburgh) at Westminster Abbey. The Jewish State of Israel was proclaimed on the 29th November by the United Nations General Assembly.

The final events of 1947 continued through December and one notable disaster took place around the 21st involving the mass migration of populations of Muslims and Hindus between Pakistan and India. Around 400,000 people died in various reciprocal murders and killings.

The review of 1947 on the whole shows it to be a relatively unremarkable one. There were ongoing conflicts, political changes, bad weather events and crashes of planes and trains. There were also births and deaths of people who are now well known or who were to become celebrities later.

The above account is only of course an outline of what happened in 1947. A detailed description can be researched from historical documents.

The sightings recorded by Kenneth Arnold focused the attention of the wider public on the existence of unidentified aerial objects. The crash at Roswell is the most famous enigmatic event to date concerning crashed UFOs and alien entities. It initiated the beginning of alleged governmental cover-ups and disinformation.

Clandestine groups were allegedly set up like the Majestic12 by Harry Truman to look into the subject of UFOs. No doubt issues such as the safety of national air space and the effectiveness of defence systems against exotic invaders were discussed.

The possibility of back-engineering advanced technology could enhance the development of human space travel. Development of new weaponry could give the USA an advantage over its rival (the Soviet Union) in the Cold War.

New technologies could be used by mankind. Acquired knowledge and understanding of alien artefacts could invigorate industrial research in new areas of research and development. Indeed there were rapid advances around the period soon after the alleged crash-retrieval at Roswell with developments involving silicon chips, optical fibres, lasers and new materials.

For sure, 1947 was the landmark year for unidentified flying objects. It represents the dawn of the modern era of investigations into the nature of UFOs and conspiracy theories.

Chapter 3
1947

Game-Changing Observations: The Maury Island Incident

Some interesting events were recorded during the same year as the crash at Roswell in 1947. There were probably three events of significance. Let's review these since they may have relevance to the famous alleged UFO crash.

An incident over Maury Island was mentioned in Chapter 2. This significant event requires further details in order to assess its importance.

Maury Island is located in the USA in the Puget Sound which is part of Washington State. It is not completely isolated. Some local homeowners decided to construct a connection with nearby Vashon Island. An isthmus was completed in 1913. The landscape is rural in nature with widespread forests though farmland is also present.

Maury Island was named after William Lewis Maury. The latter supported the *Confederate* states during the *American Civil War* and was involved in attacks on Union shipping.

The incident at Maury Island is based on the testimony of two individuals. These were Fred Crisman and Harold Dahl. They were harbour patrolmen.

According to Crisman and Dahl, debris fell from the sky on June 21st 1947 while they were out working at sea on their boat with a crew. This followed their observation of six unusual aerial objects. They described the shape of these craft as resembling doughnuts.

Debris rained down onto their boat. So what kind of material was it? Some of the matter that fell was said to be similar to volcanic lava. It resembled some form of white metal. The falling debris resulted in physical injuries. It seems that one crew member had an arm broken. An unfortunate dog was apparently killed in the incident.

Following the event, US Air Force intelligence officers from California paid Crisman and Dahl a visit. The officers were somewhat sceptical about the story. It seems that the alleged fallen material was made from a common form of aluminium. Strangely and tragically, the investigating officers did not make it back to California. They were killed in a crash.

This was not the end of the investigation into the alleged incident. There was a follow-up by the FBI. Their conclusion after questioning the witnesses was that the story was a hoax and even the claim that the two men were harbour patrolmen was fake information. However, FBI files recorded a statement from Dahl which read... "If questioned by the authorities he was going to say it was a hoax because he did not want any further trouble over the matter."

It seems that Crisman and Dahl attempted to acquire publicity and financial gain from their alleged experience. They contacted various media including newspapers and magazines. Among their contacts was a popular publication called *Fantasy Magazine*. A written report suggested that their efforts were motivated by "the hope of building up their story through publicity to a point where they could make a profitable deal with Fantasy Magazine."

It is interesting to note that Dahl claimed he was warned not to tell people about the experience or spread the news. The warning came from an unknown man wearing black clothes including a black suit... a *man in black*.

The concept of strange aerial craft as UFOs (rather than flying saucers) may have been initiated by Raymond A. Palmer. He began a publication called *Fate Magazine* in 1948. This included an article by Kenneth Arnold who became well known for his sightings of unidentified objects flying over the Cascade Mountains. Arnold was well-versed in the account of the Maury Island incident. The alleged incident at Maury Island may have generated a historical legacy.

Various books were published related to the incident and a film made in 2014 called *The Maury Island Incident.* The incident was acknowledged in 2017 by the State Senate in Washington.

Chapter 4
1947

Game-Changing Observations:Richard Rankin

Richard Rankin had considerable experience of flying – over 7,000 hours. He was familiar with observing the sky but he was not prepared for what he saw on June 23rd 1947 over Bakersfield in California. Ten mysterious craft passed by in formation flying north. They later returned, travelling in a southerly direction but this time he could only see seven objects. Rankin estimated the speed of these strange objects as ''maybe 300 to 400 miles an hour.''

So how did these sightings come about? He had been resting on his lawn taking in the sunshine. His back had been injured in a car accident so he was taking the opportunity to relax.

The objects which passed overhead did not look like conventional planes that he was familiar with. They resembled silvery discs with their lower sections rather flattened. Strangely, he could not make out any conventional structures like wings or propellers which were normal for aircraft of the time.

Whatever these objects were, they seemed to be flying in a definite formation. One object appeared to be travelling behind the others. The remaining objects were arranged in a V shape. Using his flying experience he was able to deduce an approximate height for these objects. His educated guess was around 9,000 feet.

Rankin was unsure as to what he was observing in the sky. He thought that he might have seen a prototype Navy fighter known by a nickname as the *Flying Flapjack*. However, it seems that this new aircraft probably never actually flew and definitely had not left its Connecticut base area. In fact the whole developmental programme of this new aircraft became cancelled. Work on this new plane ceased completely in March 1947.

Over the years people that have viewed inexplicable aerial objects and those that claim to have had close encounters with alien beings or even physical abductions have been very reluctant to make their experiences public. In some cases revealing information would involve breaking military or governmental protocols and sworn oaths relating to national security and put the person or their family at risk. Some revelations of information in these areas have leaked out from deathbed confessions and the introduction of the *Freedom of Information Act*.

Many reports have been made anecdotally however, and recordings of unidentified objects made on camcorders, video cameras and so on. There have also been radar returns of objects moving at ''impossible speeds'' and changing angles of flight in ways defying inertia which would be fatal to humans. Other reports indicate that many unidentified craft seem to be able to change shape and slip into and out of visibility.

Reports have come from respected individuals whose veracity is questioned by few. There are reports from pilots, military staff, police and so on. Even various Presidents have reported UFO experiences. *(Examples are discussed in my book UFO Sightings and Alien Abductions).*

What would be the motive for making false UFO sighting claims? Perhaps notoriety, fame and publicity would be enough motivation to generate falsehood as well as possible financial enrichment. There is no doubt that the whole subject area has included hoaxed cases and misidentified objects. However, a residual number of cases are totally inexplicable. The whole subject area is enigmatic.

Why would a professional person such as a policeman take the risk of declaring a UFO sighting, as with the case of police Sergeant Lonnie Zamora on Friday 24th April in 1964? He observed a landed egg-shaped craft resting on four legs in New Mexico at Socorro in the Middle Rio Grande Basin. He even observed strange insignia on the craft which in due course lifted up off the ground with a roar. It then flew off quickly without noise and leaving no smoke. Zamora went back to his vehicle and radioed a report to the Sheriff's office.

People filing reports like that of Zamora may be accused of delusion or to have mental health problems. They may be at risk of losing their jobs. Pilots who have declared sightings have in some cases been removed from their flying duties or been told to stay quiet and assume that nothing happened.

Richard Rankin similarly did not wish to be declared a crazy person. He held back on reporting his observations until other reports surfaced.

Chapter 5
1947

Game-Changing Observations:Kenneth Arnold

Perhaps the most important person to spark widespread interest in the current area of studying the UFO enigma is Kenneth Arnold.

Kenneth Albert Arnold was born on March 29th 1915. For a long period of his adult life he was a pilot and businessman. His birthplace was a town in Minnesota called *Sebeka.* Arnold had four daughters with his wife Doris until he passed away with colon cancer at 68 years old. His sad passing occurred on January 16th 1984 at the *Bellevue Hospital* in Washington.

Arnold's early life was not especially eventful. He had some interest in sport and played American football at Minnesota University. In later life he became active in the business world. Arnold formed a company involved with fire control. *The Great Western Fire Control Supply Company* took up a lot of Arnold's time in the early 1940s.

Arnold flew business trips to the area within the eastern Rocky Mountains and western Pacific. A broad part of this zone includes Canadian British Columbia and states in the USA such as Oregon, Idaho and Washington, though the confines are wider. This loose geographical area is often called the Pacific Northwest or Cascadia.

Kenneth Arnold was not a rookie aviator. He is known to have accumulated over 9,000 hours flying experience. He was familiar with observing the skies and determining the nature of viewed objects and he was well aware of the locations over which he passed. Arnold gradually became involved with aerial search and rescue flights.

Arnold became interested in running for public office. In 1962, he apparently achieved the position of Lieutenant Governor of Idaho. Prior to 1946 this position lasted for two years but it was later extended to a four year term. The office historically was introduced in 1890 which included being second in line to the State Governor.

Arnold came into the wider public gaze following a flight he made on June 24th of 1947. He reported seeing nine strange objects moving over *Mount Rainier* in Washington State. Arnold was able to give an estimated speed of the objects he had seen between 1,200 – 1,700 miles per hour. Such speeds were beyond that achievable by jet aircraft of the time. This sighting proved to be the catalyst for modern day national and international reporting of UFO sightings. It marked the beginning of a new era.

So why was Arnold on a flight? He was *en route* from *Chehalis* to *Yakima* in Washington State. The aerial flying conditions were good as he flew on his way in a Call Air A-2 aircraft on a business trip. Arnold decided on a change of plan. There had been a crash near Mount Rainier involving a US C-46 transport aircraft. There was a financial incentive to discover the wreckage to the tune of $5,000, a substantial sum of money at the time. After abandoning his search, he turned for Yakima at around 3.00 pm. He was flying at 9,200 feet high.

Something caught Arnold's eye. There was a bright flash. It was like a mirror reflecting sunlight. There was an aircraft far away moving in a different direction so he did not anticipate any aerial collision. Further bright flashes then occurred some 25 miles or so away from the direction of Mount Rainier.

Arnold observed flying objects. At first he thought he might be mistaken. He took off his eyeglasses. The window was opened and he rocked his plane. The objects were still in view. They were flying towards Mount Adams in a southerly direction.

Arnold considered the possibility that they were newly-developed jet fighters but he could not see any tails. The craft seemed to be flying in a chain-like formation. These craft appeared to have convex shapes and at least one was crescent-shaped. This shape is now associated with 'flying wings' and modern stealth aircraft. The objects moved horizontally and were spread over a distance of separation covering about five miles.

The objects that Arnold saw did not look like birds such as high-flying geese but sceptics tried to debunk Arnold's sightings. James Easton suggested the bird misidentification idea based on the presence of a local pelican population. Philip J. Klass suggested that Arnold had observed meteors. Steuart Campbell believed that temperature inversions had generated mirages of snow on the mountain peaks. In 1953, Donald Menzel suggested a number of possible explanation for Arnold's sightings including drifting clouds of snow or other types of cloud, spots of water, or reflections from his windows. None of these explanations were particularly convincing.

Arnold landed safely in Yakima at around 4 pm and reported his sighting to Al Baxter who was the airport's general manager. He later continued flying to a new destination at Pendleton in Oregon as he wished to attend an air show.

Arnold's account spread among friends and former military pilots (some of whom had experienced strange unidentified wartime *foo fighters*). Reporters interviewed Arnold on June 25th for the *East Oregonian* newspaper in Pendleton. They found him to be a credible witness.

Arnold gradually became an increasingly public figure and he seems to have tired of this. He had concerns about the pressure that the publicity would put on his marriage. He became subject to a variety of comments and mockery from some members of the public. One woman purportedly called him "the man who saw the men from Mars." A preacher said that the observed objects were "harbingers of doomsday" and advised his congregation to get ready for "the end of the world."

It was fateful that Arnold was to describe the movements of the objects he saw as resembling *saucers skipping on water*. The objects weaved and flipped through the mountain peaks. He told the *Idaho Statesman* on the 27th June in Boise that "I saw what I saw. No one can change my mind."

This resulted in subsequent press coverage which referred to what Arnold had seen as *flying saucers* and *flying discs* for the first time. The new terminology probably began around June 25th, June 26th or June 27th when Arnold's sightings were reported in Canadian, American and overseas newspapers. These days such objects are called *UFOs* (unidentified flying objects). Other descriptions made by Arnold described these objects in terms of half-moons, flat pie pans and bat-shaped.

Arnold considered various explanations of what he had seen including the possibility of the aerial objects being extraterrestrial craft. He was concerned that the public would become disturbed by such a revelation and he requested the government to disclose what these objects were that he had seen (if they knew). He bought himself a movie camera to take with him on future flights in case he had similar sightings again. The film would provide visual evidence of his veracity.

There was a degree of corroboration of Arnold's sightings. A prospector named Fred Johnson claimed to have seen six objects through his telescope from Mount Adams. L.G Bernier wrote to the *Portland Oregon Journal* claiming that he observed three of the objects over Richland in Washington State. There were around 16 reports of UFO sightings on the day of Arnold's sighting reported in the Washington State area.

A similar sighting was claimed by the crew of a United Airlines flight. This took place on July 4th. The plane was travelling from Idaho to Seattle. Nine disc-shaped craft were briefly seen.

The US military denied that the objects seen were any of their aircraft. However, the Army Air Force did make an estimate of the size of the craft which were suggested to be between 140 – 280 feet long.

Arnold was interviewed by Lieutenant Frank Brown and Captain William Davidson on July 12th at California's *Hamilton Field.* He drew annotated sketches of the nine craft that he saw. The motion of the craft reminded him of the movements of a *Chinese kite* in the wind. The interviewers concluded that Arnold had integrity and believed in what he had allegedly seen. Nevertheless, they dismissed his account as a 'mirage'.

The following image of the headline news comes from the Chicago Sun, June 26th 1947.

PAGE 2 THE CHICAGO SUN, THURSDAY, JUNE 26, 1947

In These United States

Supersonic Flying Saucers Sighted by Idaho Pilot

Speed Estimated at 1,200 Miles an Hour When Seen 10,000 Feet Up Near Mt. Rainier

PENDLETON, Ore., June 25.—(AP)

NINE bright, saucer-like objects flying at "incredible" speed at 10,000 feet altitude were reported here today by Kenneth Arnold, [illegible], pilot, who said he could not hazard a guess as to what they were.

Arnold, a U.S. Forest Service employee searching for a missing plane, said he sighted the mystery craft yesterday at 3 p.m. They were flying between Mount Rainier and Mount Adams, in Washington state, he said, and appeared to weave in and out of formation. Arnold said he clocked them and estimated their speed at 1,200 miles an hour.

Inquiries at Yakima last night brought only blank stares, he said, but he added he talked today with an unidentified man from Ukiah, south of here, who said he had seen similar objects over the mountains near Ukiah yesterday.

"It seems impossible," Arnold said, "but there it is."

* * *

Kenneth Arnold

Chapter 6
1947

The Roswell Crash

Chaves County is the location of a city in south-east New Mexico USA which was to gain notoriety and become famous worldwide. This city is Roswell. The area in current times houses a military institute and has a nearby wildlife refuge and state park. It is located seven miles from the *Pecos River*.

A UFO incident occurred in 1947 at an alleged crash site located not far from the city of Roswell on ranchland. Roswell nowadays has a healthy tourist industry and is a popular destination for visitors interested in alien beings and spacecraft as various museums and businesses abound related to these enigmatic subject areas.

The location where Roswell is now situated probably first began to become settled around 1865 with the arrival of Hispanic pioneers who arrived from Missouri. They quickly found the land to be very arid. Nevertheless, various ranches gradually became established and in 1873 Van C. Smith became the local postmaster. His father was a lawyer named Roswell Smith and this is the source of the city's name. Roswell gradually expanded with the discovery of an aquifer in 1890 and the arrival of a railway line in 1893.

So what is the 'Roswell incident'? Well, an object of some type definitely crashed.

The main event occurred when *something* crashed on ranchland 30 miles north of Roswell. The date of this landmark incident was June 14th 1947. A foreman who worked at J.B.Foster's homestead named William Brazel located the crashed object along with a considerable amount of debris.

Brazel may have collected some of the debris and hidden it under a bush to preserve it. Some reports suggest that Brazel returned to the crash site with his wife along with his daughter and son. Some investigators have put this date at around July 4th.

Brazel decided to alert a local sheriff to inform him of his discovery. The date of this is unclear but reports suggest that it was around July 6th - July 7th. It was not long before sheriff Wilcox was alerted to the discovery. Brazel thought that he might have found the remains of a crashed flying disc. He "whispered kinda confidential like" and told the law officer about his discovery. The sheriff decided to contact the Roswell Army Air Force (RAAF) to inform them of the incident.

Sheriff Wilcox was put in touch with Major Jesse Marcel at the military base. Following their discussion, Marcel assigned Lt. Colonel Sheridan Cavitt and Master Sergeant William Rickett to join him in investigations. The officers met up with Brazel and they went to the ranch area where pieces of wreckage were picked up. It appears that wreckage was strewn over some distance. The exact date of this visit is uncertain as mentioned above but it was around July 7th. They spent some time looking for further debris and did find some.

Sometime after the discovery of the wreckage Brazel informed the local *Roswell Daily Record* that (along with his son) they had come across a "large area of bright wreckage made up of rubber strips, tinfoil, a rather tough paper and sticks."

The RAAF public information officer Walter Haut issued a press release in the Roswell Daily Record on July 8th stating that personnel from the field's 509th Operation Group had recovered a *flying disc* which had crashed on a ranch near Roswell. The RAAF press release was picked up by other agencies and the word spread fast both near and far.

Samples of debris were obtained by Major Marcel. Jesse Antoine Marcel was one of the main witnesses to the event at Roswell. He was born in Terrebonne Parrish in Louisiana in 1907. His career spanned a range of employment at the Department of Transportation, US Engineers in the Army Air Corps and Shell Oil. His experience ranged from working as a draftsman to making maps. He also had spells in the US National Guard.

In March of 1942 Marcel became a 2nd Lieutenant in the US Army Air Force and he saw combat with the 5th Bomber Command in the southwest Pacific. His skills were used to analyse aerial photographs and in the area of intelligence. Marcel was awarded various military medals and rose to the rank of Major in May of 1945. After the war, he arrived at the Roswell Army Air Force base around January of 1946. Marcel continued in military service until ceasing active duty in 1950. He died in 1986. His death in Helena (Montana) was made public by his daughter Denice.

It seems that Marcel showed some of the retrieved debris to a few individuals including his son Jesse A. Marcel Jr. The material was very unusual and was not recognisable as contemporary. It showed unusual features, Marcel's son claimed that items included wreckage of foil that could not be burned or cut and sprang back into shape if crumpled up. There were also hieroglyphic-like images with a purple colouration on parts of the debris recovered from the crash.

It now transpires that there may in fact have been two crashes at sites a few miles apart. These incidents may or may not be related.

The possibility of two crash sites was suggested in press coverage based on information from an Air Force Lieutenant Colonel named Richard French some years after the crash. He was based at Alamagordo in 1947. According to French, the first UFO was downed by a US aircraft flying from *White Sands Proving Grounds* airbase which disabled the craft with an electromagnetic pulse. A retrieval attempt was made in order to recover any alien technology, debris and survivors. French claimed to have seen photos of the second crashed UFO. The craft apparently had exotic inscriptions on it.

Image of the headline news in the Roswell Daily Record in early July 1947

Leased Wire
Associated Press

Roswell Daily Record

RECORD PHONES
Business Office 2288
News Department 2287

ROSWELL, NEW MEXICO, TUESDAY, JULY 8, 1947

RAAF Captures Flying Saucer On Ranch in Roswell Region

Movies as Usual

Levees broke and flood waters rolled into the town of Grand Tower, Ill., but while the manager of the movie theater sweeps out the water that has entered the lobby these youngsters are standing in line for tickets for the night's performance. (AP Wirephoto).

Claims Army Is Stacking Courts Martial

Indiana Senator Lays Protest Before Patterson

House Passes Tax Slash by Large Margin

Defeat Amendment By Demos to Remove Many From Rolls

Security Council Paves Way to Talks On Arms Reductions

No Details of Flying Disk Are Revealed

Roswell Hardware Man and Wife Report Disk Seen

Ex-King Carol Weds Mme. Lupescu

Former King Carol of Romania and Mme. Elena Lupescu relax aboard the S. S. America bound for Cuba and Mexico in May, 1941. A member of Carol's household in Rio de Janeiro said the ex-king and his companion for 23 years in reign and exile were recently married at their hotel Copacabana Palace suite. (AP Wirephoto).

Some of Soviet Satellites May Attend Paris Meeting

Roswellians Have Differing Opinions On Flying Saucers

American League Wins All-Star Game

Miners and Operators Sign Highest Wage Pact in History

Chapter 7

Changing the Story

It should be borne in mind that in 1947, World War 2 had only come to an end two years previously. The threat of the German Nazi Third Reich was over. Hitler and Mussolini were dead. In the east, the Japanese Empire had been defeated. This inevitable outcome had been hastened by the dropping of atomic bombs on the unfortunate civilians living in Hiroshima and Nagasaki.

There were now new global tensions. The western and eastern blocs had formed. Rivalry existed between the USA and its allies and countries like the Soviet Union and her acolytes.

It was more than rivalry. There was a distinct ideological parting of the ways. The ethos of living under the rule of democracy and capitalism was far removed than that of communism and totalitarianism. A range of issues existed over new border claims and gains and the acquisition of territory. Each side was suspicious of the other. Berlin was split in half into western and eastern zones. A great wall divided the city in two. The *iron curtain* had come into being. There was a new *Cold War.*

During the war, pilots on both sides had been pursued by mysterious balls of light called *foo fighters*. They were seen in the skies in all the theatres of war. The name derived from the US 415th Night Fighter Squadron whose pilots described seeing UFOs. These strange objects manoeuvred around aircraft in what appeared to be an intelligently-controlled manner.

These foo fighters were sometimes assumed to be new kinds of devices produced by the enemy. Perhaps they were craft, maybe they were new weapons. In fact, the nature of foo fighters remains unknown, even today.

Various explanations to explain foo fighters were attempted. For example, such an attempt was made by the *Robertson Panel*. This scientific committee convened in January 1953. It was chaired by Howard P. Robertson who had made contributions to the subject of Cosmology. He was a well-known Mathematician and Physicist.

One suggestion was that foo fighters were representations of light reflecting from icy crystals. A more complex suggestion related to an uncommon electromagnetic phenomenon now called *St. Elmo's Fire.*

The occurrence of a crash in the Roswell area set off a chain of events. There was a response by the military who attended in numbers. It happened at a time when the political atmosphere was one of suspicion and mistrust. Each side was immersed in ways to overcome or dominate the other either with new discoveries, advances in technology or purely with propaganda.

The *Space Race* evolved from the competition between the USA and USSR. It was eventually won by the Soviets. *Sputnik 1* was launched on 4th October 1957. It remained in orbit for three weeks before dropping back to Earth through the atmosphere. In 1961, Yuri Gagarin was launched into orbit in *Vostok 1* on April 12th. The Soviets proclaimed him as their "sailor of the Universe."

From this background came secrecy and espionage. The legacy of the foo fighters embedded the idea that *the other side* might have newly advanced technology. There was a need to gain an advantage.

If alien technology had been recovered in the crash at Roswell, it was possible that it could be reverse-engineered. Perhaps new weapons could be made. There could be novel discoveries in the use of energy or propulsive mechanisms. Common sense suggests that the USA would not wish to hand over its discoveries to its rivals in the eastern bloc.

Since the alleged UFO crash and retrieval at Roswell, numerous conspiracy theories have abounded. These include:

- The generation of disinformation (*Projects Sign, Grudge* and to some extent, *Blue Book*)

- Secret military installations carrying out UFO research and the housing of alien beings (such as at *Area 51* in Nevada, *Dulce Base* in New Mexico and others)

- The existence of secret committees (like *Majestic 12*)

- Adversarial government agents seeking those who have seen UFOs and subsequently warning them to keep their observations secret (*Men in Black*)

- The contracting out of secret projects to companies in order to avoid public Freedom of Information Act enquiries (*Skunk Works* – the *Lockheed* company).

In the light of this background it seems that the Roswell crash initiated governmental cover-ups which have continued up until the present time.

The story of the capture of a flying disc was given to the press and this news rapidly spread worldwide. Presumably the initial information was released to the papers and media of the time in good faith. It seems likely that the military establishment quickly realised that it was a mistake to allow this information out into the public domain. It was a naïve action.

The retrieval of an alien spacecraft and possible alien entities was not purely an issue for local interest. It could have immense implications not just for cohesion in society (such as religious beliefs) but also for technological advancement over the enemies of the USA. It was essential that the US should keep any advantages that this event could confer to itself.

There was a need to deny the original story. Perhaps it was better to change the story and give out a feasible cover version. This might be more believable than a straight denial of the incident having occurred. Before looking at the change of the news release about the crashed craft, let's briefly take a look at the historical context.

It is uncertain as to how far up the chain of command the news of the crash spread. It may have gone to the very top. At the time of the incident, President H. Truman was in office in the USA. He later became a rather controversial figure to those who take an interest in the historical study of UFOs.

Truman may have been involved with setting up the Majestic 12 committee mentioned above in 1947. It is suggested that a clandestine group of selected individuals was given the task of evaluating, investigating and instigating the recovery and study of downed or crashed exotic craft. Documents relating to this were leaked in 1984.

For the research information only of interested readers, a list is given below of the names of people supposedly coerced onto this initial Majestic 12 committee. No details are attempted here. If readers would like to know more about the persons concerned and their backgrounds, they can be researched from the internet and other historical sources.

List based on Wikipedia.

- Lloyd Berkner
- Detlev Bronk
- Vannevar Bush
- James Forrestal
- Gordon Gray
- Roscoe H. Hillenkoetter
- Jerome Clarke Hunsaker
- Donald H. Menzel
- Robert M. Montague
- Sidney Souers
- Nathan F. Twining
- Hoyt Vandenberg

Project Sign was probably the first US governmental study of UFOs. It came into existence during 1948 (following its initial inauguration as *Project Saucer*). There were fears that unknown craft might represent a national security concern. Project Sign ended in 1949 and was replaced by *Project Grudge* in February 1949. This programme operated on the basis of a debunking directive. Some so-called UFO explanations defied logic and common sense. Only one formal report was published.

In March 1952, Project Grudge was in turn replaced by *Project Blue Book.* Astronomer Dr J. Allen Hynek (who was the creator of the categories of *close encounters* still used today) was the scientific consultant. The project ended officially in January 1970. 12,618 UFO reports had been made. Most were put down to misidentifications of natural phenomena (some may have been hoaxes) but a tiny proportion could not be explained.

The above projects were active during the term of President Truman. He is believed at one point to have ordered UFOs to be shot down after several were seen in the skies over the capital in 1952. However, this order was withdrawn. Prominent scientists such as Albert Einstein suggested that it was not a good idea to embark upon military conflict with craft of unspecified advanced technological design. Later investigations into UFOs took place under the auspices of the *Robertson Panel* in 1953 (mentioned previously) and the subsequent *Durant Report.*

So what changes were made to the initial press release regarding the crash of an object at Roswell? Roger Ramey was the commanding General of the Eighth Air Force at this time. Soon after the earlier report of the crash in the press he announced at a press conference that in fact the object which had crashed to the ground was in fact… *a weather balloon.*

In order to back up this assertion that a common weather balloon had crashed, debris was shown to a gathering of the press. This consisted of pieces of foil, rubber and wood.

Looking back at the crash incident now brings a lot of controversial argument to the fore. Let's start with the credibility of the main witness, Major Jesse Marcel.

Marcel's background has already been described. He had a distinguished career and appears to be a person with integrity. According to Marcel, he was ordered not to reveal his involvement with the crashed Roswell craft. His story did leak out in 1978 when it came to the attention of Stanton Friedman. This is discussed later.

Marcel's wife Linda vouched for the truthfulness of her husband's story.

"He was credible. He wasn't lying. He never embellished, only told what he saw."

"They looked through the pieces, tried to make sense of it."

"They were told to keep it quiet and they did for years and years and years."

The debris "was not of this Earth."

Denice Marcel reported that her dad told her "If we are the only ones here then there is an awful lot of wasted space out there." He wanted everyone to know that he had not made up his story and the cover-up which followed the event should cease.

Jesse's son (Jesse Marcel Jr.) graduated from medical school in Louisiana in 1961. His later career was spent in the US Navy and as a National Guard in the Army. He undertook surgical work and rose to the rank of Colonel.

Marcel Jr. claimed that the Roswell wreckage had been switched. His dad had woken him from his sleep during the night. He wanted to show him some unusual items he had brought home from a crash site that he would never get the chance to see again in the future. The material put on display later which was shown to the press following the announcement that a weather balloon had crashed was unlike the items he had seen and touched.

The so-called crashed weather balloon had held a discoid structure in place. This description was in a telex transmitted to the *FBI* (Federal Bureau of Investigation). This idea is also mentioned again in Chapter 8.

The possibility that the crashed object at Roswell was an extraterrestrial craft has been the subject of controversy for many years. This version of the story has been debunked and mocked. It is known that the military establishment wished to remove the attention of the global public away from the crash incident in 1947.

A commonly-held belief is that the wreckage came from a weather balloon. It is not substantiated that the crashed object was a weather balloon at all but if it was it later emerged that this may not have been a 'normal' one. It seems that the crashed object was a device used for espionage during the Cold War. It was a *Project Mogul* balloon. This may or may not have been the case.

If the crashed object was in fact extraterrestrial, the government and military would have been keen to distract public attention so that technological advantages for the USA might be obtained and become usable in weaponry, propulsion and so on. This could be achieved by covert back-engineering the alien technology. It would not be wise to make this available to the USA's enemies. Let's briefly look at the extraterrestrial hypothesis in a bit more detail.

The above viewpoint is supported by controversial claims made by people such as Robert 'Bob' Lazar. He supposedly worked as a scientist and engineer on a US above top secret programme during 1988 and 1989. He said he was based near Groom Lake, Nevada at the Area 51 test facility. He was located not far from Papoose Lake located in a designation called S4.

Lazar said that he was told that should he reveal information about the research he was involved with, he or his family would be executed. He was given access to a crashed extraterrestrial craft for the purpose of reverse-engineering the technology. Lazar claimed that the craft created a gravitational pull and the fabric of time and space was drawn towards it.

An element with the atomic number 115 called *Ununpentium* released antimatter particles and generated large amounts of energy. Lazar said he had seen not one but nine different extraterrestrial vehicles. He was briefed about *grey aliens* from the *zeta reticuli* star system who have been visiting the Earth for 100,000 years.

A retired mechanical engineer from Las Vegas called Bill Uhouse claimed to have been involved in back-engineering alien antigravity technology at various governmental facilities at Los Alamos and at Area 51 in Nevada. This supposedly followed the crash of an alien craft in 1953 in Arizona. Four entities were recovered and their craft loaded onto a truck and taken to a Nevada military test site north of Las Vegas.

Humans that entered the alien craft became sick. Two of the retrieved beings were injured, one seriously. They were taken to a medical facility and one survived. This entity was named *J-rod* and is mentioned in Chapter 8 along with further comments on Uhouse who passed away in 2009.

If the object that crashed at Roswell was in fact a Project Mogul balloon, this also was best kept out of the news. The military had kept the role of this programme secret because it was involved in espionage. Its role included nuclear test monitoring.

One thing is clear. The early announcement by the military that a weather balloon had crashed efficiently changed the public's perception of the event. Interest in the crash quickly waned and disappeared until the issue re-surfaced some years later. This began in the late 1970s. The subject has been a matter of controversy ever since and is discussed again later in this book.

Before leaving the topic of Project Mogul, let's briefly look at the facts about this project. What exactly was it? Why would the US government want to keep this operation out of the news and initially refer only to a weather balloon?

Project Mogul began its life as a top secret initiative. The US military held a key role in its operation and monitoring. Basically, Mogul balloons were flown at high altitudes with disc microphones which could record sound waves generated far away. Radio transmitters forwarded any recordings to ground controllers.

The idea was that the system could look for any explosions caused by atomic bomb trials carried out by the Soviet Union. It seems that the operation of these balloons continued from 1947 to 1949 after which the technology became outdated because of new seismic recording systems. The balloons used in the early days contained rubber and wood but later versions incorporated polyethylene plastics.

Clearly, the US military would not have liked to reveal their espionage activities to their Cold War opponents in the Soviet Union. However, if the material found in the wreckage at Roswell did in fact consist of a crashed UFO, then that would also have been of benefit to the USA and keeping it out of the news would be sensible. It could enhance the study of advanced technology. Once again, secrecy would have been paramount.

Major Jesse Marcel with Roswell crash debris

Disk Craze Continues

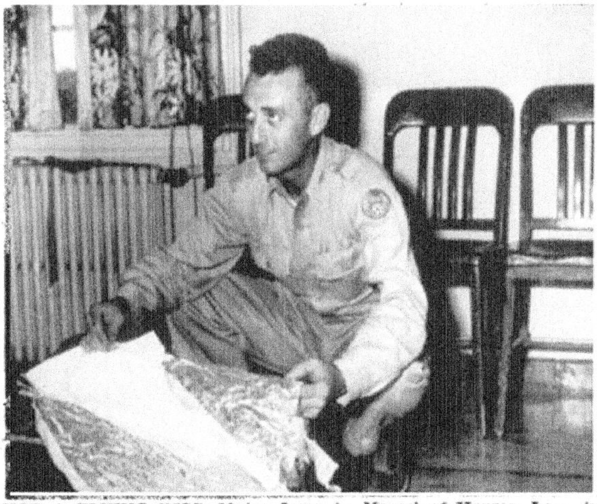

NOT A FLYING DISC—Major Jesse A. Marcel of Houma, La., intelligence officer of the 509th Bomb Group at Roswell, New Mexico, inspects what was identified by a Fort Worth, Texas, Army Air Base weather forecaster as a ray wind target used to determine the direction and velocity of winds at high altitudes. Initial stories originating from Roswell, where the object was found, had labelled it a "flying disc" but inspection at Fort Worth revealed its true nature. (AP Wirephoto).

Army Disk-ounts New Mexico Find As Weather Gear

FORT WORTH, July 9.—(AP)—An examination by the Army revealed last night that a mysterious object found on a lonely New Mexico ranch was a harmless high-altitude weather balloon—not a grounded flying disk.

Excitement was high in disk-conscious Texas until Brig Gen. Roger M. Ramey, commander of the Eight Air Forces with headquarters here cleared up the mystery.

The bundle of tinfoil, broken wood beams and rubber remnants of a ballon was sent here yesterday by army air transport in the wake of reports that it was a flying disk.

But the general said the objects were the crushed remains of a Ray wind target used to determine the direction and velocity of winds at high altitudes.

Warrant Officer Irving Newton, forecaster at the Army Air Forces weather station here, said "we use them because they go much higher than the eye can see."

LOST PURSE HOLDING DIAMONDS IS FOUND, BUT MONEY MISSING

Somewhere in Corsicana Wed-

Chapter 8

The Retrieval

The ranch site of the crash at Roswell did not have telephone communication. This may explain any delay in contacting the local sheriff after the discovery of the wreckage. However, soon after being alerted about the crash site, the remains were retrieved by the military and initially taken to the Roswell Army Air Field. This is where early inspection of the debris began.

There was rapid communication between military staff. The commanding officer of the 509th Operations Group Eighth Air Force at Roswell during this time was Colonel William H. Blanchard. He liaised with the Eighth Air Force located in Fort Worth (Texas). Accounts suggest that in due course the crashed disc was loaded onto a truck. This was not the final outcome or the end-destination of the wrecked object. General Roger M. Ramey instructed that the wreckage should be transferred. It was to be flown to Fort Worth for further inspection.

Fort Worth itself was not to be the final destination of the crash debris. A B29 bomber with the wreckage continued onwards to Wright-Field (later called Wright-Patterson) Air Force Base in Dayton, Ohio. After the arrival of the wreckage it seems that General Ramey took over the control of events and it is said that a suspected cover-up of the true nature of the craft began which lasted for the rest of the century right up to the present time.

The alleged cover-up story suggested that the crashed and retrieved material was a weather balloon. It may have had a reflective tracking device attached to it called a *kite*. This was a view expressed by various personnel including a certain Warrant Officer Irving Newton.

In fact, the wreckage may not have come from a basic weather balloon. It could in fact have been a crashed Project Mogul espionage device. This was discussed in Chapter 7. Alternatively, it could have been a downed alien spacecraft.

There were witness reports that the crashed object not only consisted of the remains of an exotic craft but also claimed that alien bodies were recovered by the military and removed for examination. There were supposedly 3 or 4 such entities. They were described as appearing small – shorter than humans, maybe 3 or 4 feet tall, slender with spindly limbs, relatively large bald heads and with slanting eyes on their faces. These days they would be referred to as 'grey aliens'. It may be that at least one individual was recovered alive and lived for some time at a secret location.

The above claim generated various controversies some of which involved dubious veracity. Arguments followed over the years for and against a range of claims and revelations.

In the 1990s, London-based Ray Santilli released a seventeen minute black and white film which purported to show an authentic alien autopsy. The alien body was supposedly that of a being recovered from the crashed disc at Roswell in 1947. Santilli said that he had got hold of the film through an anonymous retired military cameraman.

Bill Uhouse claimed that a survivor of an extraterrestrial crash similar to the event at Roswell occurred near Kingman in Arizona during 1953. This resulted in liaison with a live surviving entity named *J-rod.* This individual suffered from cell deterioration and was maintained at a facility five floors under the Papoose Mountain in a specially created survival area in the S4 region of Area 51 in Nevada.

A purported document supposedly reported on tissue samples taken from J-rod to the Majestic 12 group said to have been set up by President Harry S. Truman in 1947 (tasked to research the crashed disc and non-human bodies from the Roswell incident).

J-rod had the appearance of what is now known as a *grey alien*. The entity was reported to be 200 years old. Dan Burisch claimed to have interviewed J-rod but said he was not an extraterrestrial but a visitor from the distant future.

The recovery of alien bodies live or dead from the Roswell site is one of hot debate. There is some supporting evidence but once again the veracity of this has been questioned.

Glenn Dennis was born in 1925 on March 24th and passed away on April 28th 2015. He attended Roswell High School. Dennis worked for a brief time at the *Ballard Funeral Home* starting around 1940. He washed the hearse and also learned about embalming. Later, he graduated from the San Francisco *College of Mortuary Science*. This was on 22nd December in 1946.

Dennis went back to the Ballard Funeral Home in 1946. He was awarded a contract with the US Army Air Force and transported corpses and injured personnel in his ambulance. He frequently liaised with the Roswell Army Air Field (RAAF) base.

Among the areas of interest relating to Dennis is that he was one of the founders of the *UFO Museum and Research Centre* in Roswell and claimed to have witnessed alien bodies and crashed wreckage.

Dennis said that he received a phone call from the military base. He was asked whether he had any small caskets. The caller was interested in baby caskets 3 - 4 feet in size and hermetically sealed. Apparently Dennis had two, one in storage and another on display. The caller wanted more. A further call enquired about how to maintain a body while keeping its chemical nature intact. There was a discussion about embalming fluids.

The same day Dennis was called out to transfer an injured member of the base to hospital. Dennis claims to have observed a shiny object looking like it was made of stainless steel in a field ambulance. Some parts of the object looked black but he could also make out pink and purple regions. Dennis claimed that he spoke to an officer and asked him about the object. The latter became angry and had him removed from the base by military police.

Dennis had a coffee the next day with a nurse known to him who had apparently also been at the base. She appeared upset. According to Dennis, she sketched some entities she had seen onto a napkin. They were bizarre. Their eyes were prominent and situated on large heads. As for their fingers, they only had four. The fingers appeared to have structures on them that might have been used for extra grip or suction. According to Dennis, he kept these drawings in a cabinet in his place of work. At some point the latter was discarded and the drawings lost.

If the story about supplying small caskets is true and also his observations of a crashed object and the account made by the nurse, Dennis kept it all secret for a very long time. He is said to have stated…

"I didn't talk about it until 1990. I just didn't want to get involved in it. I never told my wife or anybody else. If I'd told this in 1947, who would have believed it anyway? I didn't want my kids getting made fun of because their old man saw flying things."

Many witnesses of UFO sightings, landings or other encounters often do not report or talk about their experiences. It seems some have been intimidated by the military and have been told to stay quiet. Retribution has been threatened both to the witnesses and their families. This has been done by regular military personnel or sometimes by mysterious undesignated *Men in Black*.

The prospect of future job promotion could be put at risk or even the outcome of sacking and removal from the workplace might result should the witness speak out. The witness may also be subjected to ridicule or be diagnosed with mental illness ranging from delusions, hallucinations to paranoia. Psychiatric referral may be deemed necessary.

In some cases though, regression hypnosis has revealed strange memories as exemplified by the alleged abducted married couple Betty and Barney Hill in 1961. They claimed to have been abducted from their car in a rural area of New Hampshire. Having seen a moving bright light in the sky at 10-30 pm, their way was blocked by a landed vehicle and they were taken on board by humanoid figures and subjected to medical examinations against their will. They later found themselves some distance along their route home and had experienced missing time.

Their disturbing dreams led them to be referred to Dr Benjamin Simon in Boston and both the Hills independently told a similar story of the abduction event while undergoing regression hypnosis. The abductors were described as grey aliens from the *zeta reticuli* constellation.

Sometimes information about UFO encounters has come to light many years after the actual event. In many cases this has occurred when the witness reaches a point in life where disclosure of information no longer matters to them or the consequences are not feared. In some cases deathbed confessions have been made or the contents of sealed documents revealed. Let's mention a couple of case studies.

Paul Theodore Hellyer became the *Minister of National Defence* after a Canadian election victory in 1963. He announced his belief in UFOs in 2007 and demanded that world governments should disclose their knowledge of alien technology. Hellyer claimed that aliens live among the human population and they had worked with the USA government. He also claimed that four or more different species of aliens have been visiting planet Earth for thousands of years.

A deathbed revelation has been unearthed which relates directly to the Roswell incident. Lieutenant Walter Haut was mentioned in Chapter 6. He played a vital role in the event having been instructed to give out press releases to expose the details of the crash to the public via the media.

Haut passed away on December 15th 2005 at the age of 83. He left behind a sworn affidavit containing information pertaining to his experiences at Roswell. In the document he described the crashed weather balloon as a cover story. The military retrieved a craft and he saw it in a hangar and small alien bodies. This to some extent corroborates the account of undertaker Glenn Dennis who said he was asked about the supply of child-size caskets.

According to the document, Haut attended a meeting with military colleagues including Colonel William Blanchard and Air Force General Roger Ramey. They passed round pieces of wreckage and crash debris. The material was touched and examined. Nobody knew what the nature of it was. There had been two crash sites and the press release would be made in order to distract observers from visiting and disturbing the second one.

Military personnel were asked to go to both sites. Their task was to carefully search for and retrieve any further debris. All visible and physical signs of the crashes had to be removed. This was a terrestrial ''clean-up'' operation of the affected areas and no sign of remnants should be left on site.

So what did Haut actually see? The document gave quite a lot of surprising detail. Colonel Blanchard took him to a secure hangar at the Roswell base designated as *Building 84*. The hangar housed an exotic-looking craft. It had the shape of an egg. It seemed to be made of some type of metal. This object was very unconventional. Haut looked for windows, wings and landing gear but they were not present. The dimensions of the craft were surprisingly small. He estimated the length to be no more than 15 feet. As for the width, it was just some 6 feet across.

There was a further amazing revelation. Two alien bodies lay on the floor with a tarpaulin sheet partially covering them. They did not look human. They were only about 4 feet tall. Their heads were relatively large. Haut believed that the craft and its crew did not originate from planet Earth but had come from somewhere in outer space.

Chapter 9

Rediscovering the Documents

The story of the events at Roswell in 1947 became hidden and forgotten as the years passed by. However, during the 1970s, an interest in the matter was re-kindled. The subject of UFO research gained in popularity. Many researchers (too many to name here) began interviews relating to UFO events. Many witnesses were discovered who claimed to have knowledge of the incident at Roswell.

Research into UFO events became somewhat easier with the introduction of the *Freedom of Information Act*. This was incorporated into US law in 1966 and similar legislation was introduced by several other countries in later years. The records of US governmental agencies became easier to access by the public and more transparent. However, many documents had sections of them blacked out, allegedly for national security reasons.

Interviews with witnesses revealed accounts of an alien flying disc crash at Roswell. Many stories included the suggestion that not only had a craft been retrieved but also that alien bodies had been recovered. Some versions of accounts say that about eight aliens were involved in the crash. Two aliens survived but one quickly died. The other was taken away by the military. The stories vary but such descriptions can be found in books such as *Crash at Corona* (1992) co-authored by Stanton Friedman.

There have been claims that there was a conspiracy by the government in order to cover-up what had really transpired. For example, suggestions were made by official sources that the recovered bodies were actually dummies being used in tests related to high altitude parachuting studies (though this seems very doubtful for the time period of the Roswell incident). A more recent suggestion is that the bodies were medically altered children made to look like aliens by the Soviets with the aim of inducing terror into American society.

Let's focus our attention on one of the key players whose research was to have an important role in bringing the Roswell affair into the public domain. This was Stanton T. Friedman.

Stanton Terry Friedman was born on July 29th 1934. He lived in Fredericton which is located in New Brunswick (Canada). He passed away due to a heart attack at the *Toronto Pearson Airport* in 2019 on May 13th.

Friedman graduated from *Linden High School* and by 1956 had gone on to gain various qualifications in nuclear physics. He had a long career in this subject area working for renowned companies such as *General Electric, Aerojet General Nucleonics, General Motors, Westinghouse, TRW* and *McDonnell Douglas*. Included among his tasks were classified research studies on nuclear-powered aircraft. He also worked on rocket systems which could make use of nuclear fission and fusion reactions. Other work was relevant to various space-research spin-off products including novel nuclear power plants.

Friedman became absorbed with the subject of UFOs. He took the sightings and reports seriously and considered them to be worthy of scientific research. With this in mind he ceased mainstream employment in 1970.

Friedman began a national programme intended to inform and educate both the general public and officialdom of the case for extraterrestrial visitation by exotic craft. His UFO agenda took him to numerous colleges and organisations in many states across the USA. His lecture tours were not confined to the US and he visited at least 19 countries. He became known as an authority on the subject of UFOs and he published many papers and guested on various radio and television shows.

Friedman stood his ground and fought his case against debunkers and sceptics vehemently for his stance on the nature of UFOs. In general, he found that the public and press were unaware of the substantive evidence for his arguments. He also criticised the nature of the *SETI* programme (*Search For Extraterrestrial Intelligence*) for relying on signal detection rather than confirmed unexplained sightings.

The status of Friedman within the scope of UFO research rose to the point where he submitted information to *Congress* and addressed the *United Nations*. He proposed that planet Earth is receiving visitation from extraterrestrial craft. This was suggested to the *House of Representatives* in the US in 1968. He even speculated about the systems allowing these craft to travel and he talked of magneto-hydrodynamic propulsion systems. It is a matter of minor interest that Friedman generally talked about flying saucers rather than UFOs.

In a debate with other guests in 2004, Friedman stated on the *Coast to Coast* radio show that UFOs originate from planets whose sun is not unlike that of the Earth. He backed up his arguments using evidence from the Betty and Barney Hill abduction event discussed elsewhere in this book. Under regression hypnosis, Betty drew a star map for astronomer Marjorie Fish. This was later said to match the constellation *zeta reticuli* 39 light years away.

Stanton Friedman achieved a lot for the advancement of the studies of UFOs. As far as Roswell is concerned, he was involved in identifying the site of the event. He took the view that the incident did involve a crash of an extraterrestrial vehicle.

Friedman communicated with Jesse Marcel Sr. during the 1970s who had seen and handled the Roswell debris. He contributed a written section to Jesse Marcel Jr's 2007 book called *The Roswell Legacy*.

Friedman went on to research and release documents in 1978 which he believed were genuine and originated from reports of the secret Majestic 12 committee set up in 1947 to study UFOs and their implications for national security.

Chapter 10

The Legacy

One unproven aspect of the Roswell legacy relates to the rapid advances in technological knowledge and inventions that occurred in the years following shortly after the crash incident. There have been claims that these developments arose as spin-offs from back-engineered Roswell debris.

The speculation about the origin of rapidly developed human technology catalysed by the Roswell event was not based entirely on rumour. It was given credence by some respected individuals. One such person was Lieutenant Philip James Corso (May 22nd 1915 - July 16th 1998).

Corso was born in Jupiter (Florida). He rose through the ranks in the American Army and became the co-author of a book called *The Day After Roswell* with William J. Birns. Corso claimed to have had a role in studying exotic technology obtained from the Roswell crash. He recounted his experiences on the radio show *Coast to Coast* with Art Bell in 1997 and again in 2010.

The full history of Corso's career will not be detailed here but he held various posts in military service including intelligence duties. Corso claimed that Admiral Roscoe H. Hillenkoetter was a member of the covert Majestic 12 committee set up to study the nature and military significance of UFOs. This group had *above top secret* status and anyone outside of the group including Presidents of the USA were kept out of the loop based on whether or not there was a *need to know*.

The secret group was tasked to collect as much information as possible on non-Earthly technology. The US government kept information away from the public gaze by any necessary means including cover-stories, misinformation and possibly intimidation.

Corso referred to various companies contracted to carry out reverse-engineering. Some of the products have been mentioned in other parts of this book but they include Kevlar material (a strong heat resistant synthetic fibre), silicon circuit chips, laser beams, accelerated particle beam equipment and fibre-optic technology. Corso also claimed that the *Strategic Defence Initiative* or *Star Wars* project was not just designed to destroy incoming enemy guided missiles. It was also to be used to disable incoming alien spaceships.

Revelations and claims were made by other individuals. Donna Hare became a whistle-blower following seven years working for NASA with a very high security clearance status. Her area of expertise focused on the study of photographs taken of satellites and also images taken on the moon. Hare claimed that she observed UFOs on NASA photos in the late 1970s and a colleague confirmed the nature of these pictures. Hare said that she was tasked to airbrush such images out of NASA photos before they were released to the media and public.

The Scot Gary McKinnon was accused of hacking US military and NASA computers in 2002. An extradition request was made to transfer McKinnon from the UK to the USA (which did not succeed - he suffered from *Asperger's Syndrome* and depression) after he claimed to have seen photos showing UFOs in the atmosphere, work on back-engineering of UFO technology, studies of antigravity propulsion systems, information about suppressed *free energy* availability and a remarkable claim to have read lists of names and ranks of *non-terrestrial officers* in the US military.

The present understanding of the immensity of the *observable Universe* has added credence to speculation by astronomers that life is likely to exist on planetary systems in star systems other than our own solar system. In 1961 Frank Drake produced an equation for the *SETI* programme (*Search For Extraterrestrial Intelligence*) which stimulated discussion among scientists. His *Drake Equation* is unproven but some have used it to quantify the number of intelligent civilisations that could exist in our *Milky Way* galaxy. The calculated number is vast. Of course, there are billions of galaxies.

There may also be a *non-observable Universe* containing objects so distant that the light has not yet reached the Earth. It may never do so as the Universe has been expanding since the *Big Bang*.

It is now speculated that many recently discovered planets are in suitable orbits around stars where conditions are just right for life to take hold. These habitable regions are called *Goldilocks Zones*.

In the 1960s and 1970s there was renewed interest in the subject of UFOs. A more scientific approach to studying the phenomena began to build. Witness interviews brought new cases to light, though of course not all of these could be taken at face value. Some reports were misidentifications or hoaxes by individuals seeking publicity.

However, the 'science' of Ufology became slightly more mainstream rather than a fringe topic though there were many myths about so-called *little green men* and public ignorance of the subject. It was often a matter of hilarity or cynicism when individuals attempted to debate the evidence.

UFO researchers like nuclear physicist Stanton T. Friedman interviewed UFO witnesses and submitted information on the subject to *Congress* and addressed the *United Nations*. He released documentation that may or may not have been genuine relating to UFO studies by the Majestic 12 group.

Friedman also reviewed various surveys. Gallup polls taken at intervals between 1966 and 1987 showed steady results indicating the belief by respondents in the general public that UFOs were real. These views were in the 60% or more range of agreement.

Industrial Research and Development polls in 1971 and 1979 produced somewhat similar results. However, when it came to the nature of UFOs, only 32% and 44% respectively of scientists who took part in the surveys felt that observed unidentified objects came from outer space beyond the boundaries of planet Earth. A high proportion of scientific respondents believed that the sightings were in one way or another caused by unusual natural events such as atypical weather conditions or atmospheric phenomena. Others did not have any clear idea as to the cause of UFO sightings.

The 1997 survey by *CNN/Time* showed that beliefs in the general population had moved on again compared to the 1970s. There was a clear majority view that the US government had covered-up a lot of information relating to UFO sightings and alien abductions. There was mistrust and many conspiracy theories aimed at officialdom. Alien beings had most likely been visiting the Earth for many years. The Roswell crash was one example of such visitation that had somehow ended in disaster for the entities concerned.

In recent times strange UFO sightings have been recorded not just as photos but also on videos and camcorders. Unexplained footage has been taken by both civil and military pilots as well as by astronauts.

The Roswell incident was the subject of a television movie made in 1994. Its full title was *Roswell: The UFO Cover-Up*. The producer was Paul Davids.

Another legacy reflected by the crash at Roswell and UFO sightings in general is the publication of articles in magazines and newspaper reports. Books abound and are far too numerous to analyse or make a comprehensive list here.

A few examples are named below for the interest of readers. Some have historical significance. Note that the first book in the list is a publication of my own.

UFO Sightings And Alien Abductions And Other Strange Events (2017) by Dr Graham Clingbine

The Day After Roswell (1997) by Philip J. Corso and William J. Birns

The Truth about the UFO Crash at Roswell (1994) by Randle and Schmitt

Crash at Corona (1992) by Stanton Friedman and Don Berliner

The Roswell Incident (1980) by Charles Berlitz and William Moore

Chapter 11

Facts and Speculation

The Roswell incident has become iconic and the events of that fateful day back in 1947 have become known globally. However, the true nature of what took place is not definitively proven. It is probably the most well-known case of a UFO encounter in history. It is only rivalled in notoriety by a few other cases. The author would cite here two other examples though they did not attain the widespread recognition that emanated from the crash site in New Mexico.

There is no space in this book to document in detail the numerous other case studies of UFO encounters so just two other controversial events are mentioned but only briefly.

The first incident occurred over two days in late December of 1980. This is the Rendlesham Forest sighting in Suffolk, England. It involved two separate observations of a landed egg-shaped craft at RAF Woodbridge (twinned with RAF Bentwaters) which was used by the US Air Force as a nuclear facility at that time. The object was examined by military personnel. A famous voice-tape recording was made by Lieutenant Colonel Charles Halt as he approached the craft through the trees.

Another controversial event occurred in 1992 which has become known as the *Phoenix Lights*. There were two sightings over Phoenix in Arizona around March 13th. Triangular craft with lights passed silently over the state, generating many calls to the police by the public. Local politicians held a press conference to try and explain the observations but initially the matter was not taken seriously. The military debunked the sightings and said that people had seen flares dropped from aircraft.

The Rendlesham Forest and Phoenix Lights events are just two cases picked out from thousands of reports and incidents documented over the years. To some extent they rival the Roswell incident but there is little doubt that the latter set in motion years of research into UFOs along with numerous conspiracy theories and public entertainment by way of books, television programmes and movies.

Let's summarise the Roswell incident and put the event into two categories.

Facts

1. An object crashed on a ranch in New Mexico around June 14th 1947.

2. Debris was left scattered on the ground.

3. Wreckage was retrieved by the military and taken away for examination.

4. A press release was issued stating that a flying disc had crashed. The details of this story were subsequently changed.

5. News of the crash received worldwide attention.

6. Since the incident there have been ongoing disputes as to the true nature of what took place including disagreements between Ufologists.

7. Pronouncements about the incident have been put out by official government sources over the years and these gave different explanations at various times.

8. There is an ongoing legacy of interest by the public which has given rise to all manner of fictional versions of the incident in movies, shows and books etc.

Speculation

1. The crashed object was a weather balloon.

2. The crashed object was a Project Mogul high altitude espionage balloon.

3. The source of the debris at Roswell came from a crashed flying saucer.

4. Wreckage material retrieved from the crashed object was made by exotic advanced technology.

5. The real crash debris was switched when shown to the public.

6. There were two separate crash sites.

7. Alien bodies (living and dead) were recovered from the crash site.

8. The entities retrieved from the crash were extraterrestrial in nature and their craft was from outer space. (Later ideas suggested that the beings were inter-dimensional or came from the distant future).

9. Retrieved bodies were in fact dummies *or* children physically altered by the Soviets to inject fear into USA society.

10. Advanced technologies and products (such as Kevlar, lasers, silicon chips and optical fibres) were invented following subsequent industrial research on materials retrieved and reverse-engineered from the crash site.

Books By Dr Graham Clingbine

Disclosure-The Future is Now... a science fiction story about how events in the distant future may come back to affect the present. Kevin is placed in a dilemma being required to choose between his daughter and the future of humanity. Author: Dr G Clingbine. 2nd Edition published by Reed UK.

Release From Stasis-The Future is Now... a science fiction novel and sequel to Disclosure set in the distant future which can be read in its own right without the need to refer to its predecessor. The protagonist John, the last surviving human, battles to save mankind using advanced genetic technology and time travel in order to overcome changes to the Earth caused by a hostile sun. His work is hindered by new astral religions in conflict with each other, the Muons and the Pions. Author: Dr G Clingbine. 2nd Edition published by AV Publishing (South Africa).

UFO Sightings And Alien Abductions (And Other Strange Events)... a review of strange aerial sightings, landings and alleged human abductions by alien entities from pre-history up to the present time. This book is a must-read for anyone interested in the subject area. In addition to well known cases such as the alleged crash at Roswell in New Mexico, the Betty and Barney Hill abduction and the conspiracy theories about activities at Area 51, numerous other cases and events are included many of which are not very well known. Author: Dr Graham Clingbine. Published by Reed UK.

The Real Roswell Incident 1947... an account of the events of the famous flying saucer crash at Roswell in New Mexico in 1947. An account is given of the crash and the alleged retrieval of an extraterrestrial craft and alien bodies. The different theories as to the nature of the debris is discussed and the issues surrounding possible governmental disinformation and cover-up stories. Author: Dr G Clingbine. Published by Reed UK.

Corona Virus: Pandemic Poems... a collection of poems outlining the events and experiences suffered globally during the pandemic spread of the corona CV-19 virus and the terrifying covid disease in 2020. Author: Dr G Clingbine: published by AV Publishing (South Africa).

A Collection of Bedtime & Daytime Stories for Children... six stories for children up to the age of 14 which challenge their imagination in a world where anything is possible. Author: Graham Clingbine PhD. Published by Reed UK.

The Network Marketing Bible... A quick essential guide for all Network Marketing and Multi-Level Marketing (MLM) Businesses – A start-up guide for beginners & good practice for potential entrepreneurs. Author : Dr G Clingbine. Published by Reed UK.

Secrets of Human Sexual Attraction: Find Your Ideal Sexual Partner... This book contains a frank non-technical review of the physiological, psychological and behavioural processes involved in human sexual attraction. Some comparisons are made between different cultural, religious and national communities. Secrets of Human Sexual Attraction is a 'must-read' for adults of all ages. The content is challenging and enlightening. Use the Quiz at the end of the book to assess your own sexuality and attractiveness.The author hopes this book will help you Find Your Ideal Sex Partner. Author Dr Graham Clingbine. Published by AV Publishing (South Africa).

What You Need To Know About Human Sex – Facing The Taboos... an easy to read and interesting review of human sexual behaviour, diversity and taboos, this book has been recommended for use by high school students, young adults and indeed adults of any age group. Author: Dr G Clingbine. 2nd Edition published by AV Publishing (South Africa).

My Autobiography: Sharing My Life Story With You... This is the intriguing life story of Graham Clingbine. You most probably have not heard of him, yet his story makes fascinating reading. Many readers look for the autobiographies of celebrities, famous or wealthy individuals. These attributes do not guarantee that their life histories will make interesting reading. This is your chance to read about the life of a 'real' person, perhaps someone you can identify with. Meet Graham's friends and family... and what they got up to. Discover his sporting interests, romances and his life passions. Find out how his life pathway produced two marriages The autobiography of Graham Clingbine steers the reader through his life story from birth along the pathway of the aging process recounting many fascinating incidents with both good and bad outcomes. Learn about his family background, health challenges, successes, failures and outlook on life. Graham is sharing his life story with YOU! Author Graham Clingbine BSc.MSc.PhD. Published by AV Publishing (South Africa).

The above books can be ordered from online platforms such as Amazon, Barnes and Noble, and Lulu, in formats such as paperbacks or ebooks.

AUTHOR WEBSITE

www.grahamclingbine.co.uk

Printed in Great Britain
by Amazon

58232643R00047